Room Nine, Kindergarten Friends

Mrs.

Junie B. Jones

Richie Lucille

That Grace

Meanie Jim

Crybaby William

Paulie Allen Puffer

Jamal Hall

Ricardo

Roger

Charlotte

Lynnie

Laugh Out Loud with Junie B. Jones!

#1 *Junie B. Jones and the Stupid Smelly Bus*

#2 *Junie B. Jones and a Little Monkey Business*

#3 *Junie B. Jones and Her Big Fat Mouth*

#4 *Junie B. Jones and Some Sneaky Peeky Spying*

#5 *Junie B. Jones and the Yucky Blucky Fruitcake*

#6 *Junie B. Jones and That Meanie Jim's Birthday*

#7 *Junie B. Jones Loves Handsome Warren*

#8 *Junie B. Jones Has a Monster Under Her Bed*

#9 *Junie B. Jones Is Not a Crook*

#10 *Junie B. Jones Is a Party Animal*

#11 *Junie B. Jones Is a Beauty Shop Guy*

#12 *Junie B. Jones Smells Something Fishy*

#13 *Junie B. Jones Is (almost) a Flower Girl*

#14 *Junie B. Jones and the Mushy Gushy Valentime*

#15 *Junie B. Jones Has a Peep in Her Pocket*

#16 *Junie B. Jones Is Captain Field Day*

#17 *Junie B. Jones Is a Graduation Girl*

#18 *Junie B. Jones: First Grader (at last!)*

#19 *Junie B. Jones: Boss of Lunch*

#20 *Junie B. Jones: Toothless Wonder*

#21 *Junie B. Jones: Cheater Pants*

#22 *Junie B. Jones: One-Man Band*

#23 *Junie B. Jones: Shipwrecked*

#24 *Junie B. Jones: BOO . . . and I MEAN It!*

#25 *Junie B. Jones: Jingle Bells, Batman Smells!
    (P.S. So Does May.)*

#26 *Junie B. Jones: Aloha-ha-ha!*

#27 *Junie B. Jones: Dumb Bunny*

#28 *Junie B. Jones: Turkeys We Have Loved
    and Eaten (and Other Thankful Stuff)*

*Junie B. Jones: Top-Secret Personal Beeswax:
    A Journal by Junie B. (and me!)*

Junie B.'s Essential Survival Guide to School

Junie B. Jones: These Puzzles Hurt My Brain! Book

Junie B. Jones: Junie B. My Valentime

junie b. jones®
and Her Big Fat Mouth

2 Books in 1!

junie b. jones®
Is a Party Animal

by BARBARA PARK

illustrated by
Denise Brunkus

A STEPPING STONE BOOK™

Random House 🏠 New York

Text copyright © 1993, 1997 by Barbara Park
Cover art and interior illustrations copyright © 1993, 1997 by Denise Brunkus

All rights reserved. Published in the United States by Random House Children's Books, a division of Penguin Random House LLC, New York. The titles in this work were originally published separately in the United States by Random House Children's Books, a division of Penguin Random House LLC, New York, in 1993 and 1997.

Random House and the colophon are registered trademarks and A Stepping Stone Book and the colophon are trademarks of Penguin Random House LLC. Junie B. Jones is a registered trademark of Barbara Park, used under license.

Visit us on the Web!
JunieBJones.com

Educators and librarians, for a variety of teaching tools, visit us at
RHTeachersLibrarians.com

The Library of Congress has cataloged the individual books under the following Control Numbers: 92050957 (*Junie B. Jones and Her Big Fat Mouth*) and 97017320 (*Junie B. Jones Is a Party Animal*).

ISBN 978-0-593-90138-0 (trade)

Printed in the United States of America
10 9 8 7 6 5 4 3 2 1

This book has been officially leveled by using the F&P Text Level Gradient™ Leveling System.

Contents

1. *Junie B. Jones
   and Her Big Fat Mouth* vii

2. *Junie B. Jones
   Is a Party Animal* 71

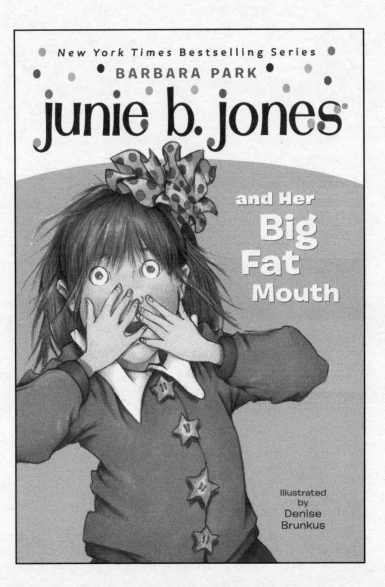

New York Times Bestselling Series
BARBARA PARK

junie b. jones®

and Her
Big
Fat
Mouth

illustrated
by
Denise
Brunkus

Contents

1. Punishment   1

2. The Cop and Dr. Smiley   12

3. Me and My Big Fat Mouth   21

4. Dumb Ollie   30

5. Shining   37

6. Tingling   46

7. Jobs and Jobs   51

8. Gus Vallony   63

1
Punishment

My name is Junie B. Jones. The B stands for Beatrice. Except I don't like Beatrice. I just like B and that's all.

I go to kindergarten. My room is named Room Nine. There are lots of rules in that place.

Like no shouting.

And no running in the hall.

And no butting the other children in the stomach with your head.

My teacher's name is Mrs.

She has another name, too. But I just like Mrs. and that's all.

Last week Mrs. clapped her loud hands together. Then she made a 'nouncement to us.

A *'nouncement* is the school word for telling us something very important.

"Boys and girls. May I have your attention, please?" she said. "Today is going to be a special day in Room Nine. We're going to be talking about different careers you can have when you grow up."

"Yeah, only guess what?" I said. "I never even heard of that dumb word careers before. And so I won't know what the heck we're talking about."

Mrs. made squinty eyes at me. "A career

is a *job*, Junie B.," she said. "And please raise your hand before you speak."

Then Mrs. talked some more about careers. And she said Monday was going to be called Job Day. And everybody in Room Nine would come to school dressed up like what kind of job they wanted to be.

After that, Room Nine was very excited. Except for not me. 'Cause I had a big problem, that's why.

"Yeah, only guess what?" I said. "I don't know what I want to be when I grow up. And so that means I can't come to school on Monday. And now I'll probably flunk kindergarten."

"Hurray!" shouted a mean boy named Jim.

I made a fist at him. "How'd you like a

knuckle sandwich, you big fat Jim?" I shouted right back.

Mrs. came over to my table. She bended down next to me.

"*Please,* Junie B. You simply must try to control yourself better in class. We've talked about this before, remember?"

"Yes," I said nicely. "Only I hate that dumb guy."

Just then my bestest friend Lucille—who sits next to me—stood up and fluffed her ruffly dress.

"I always control myself, don't I, Teacher?" she said. "That's because my nanna taught me to act like a little lady. And so Junie B. Jones should act more like me."

I made a growly face at her. "I *do* act like a little lady, you dumb bunny Lucille! And

don't say that again, or I'll knock you on your can."

Mrs. did a frown at me.

"Just kidding," I said very quick.

Except for Mrs. kept on frowning. And then she gave me punishment.

Punishment is the school word for sitting at a big table all by yourself.

And everybody keeps on staring at you.

And it makes you feel like P.U.

That's how come I put my head down on the table. And I covered it up with my arms.

'Cause punishment takes the friendly right out of you.

And so at recess I didn't speak to Lucille. And I didn't speak to my other bestest friend named Grace, either.

I just sat down in the grass all by myself.

And I watched Janitor paint the litter cans.

And I played with a stick and an ant and that's all.

"I hate Room Nine," I said very grumpity.

Except for just then I saw something very wonderful in the grass! And its name was two cherry Life Savers!

"Hey! I love those guys!" I said.

Then I quick picked one up. And I blowed off the germs. And I put it right in my mouth.

"WAIT! DON'T DO THAT!" shouted a loud voice at me. "SPIT THAT OUT RIGHT NOW!"

I turned my head.

It was Janitor! He was running at me speedy quick. His jingly keys were jangling all

over the place.

"SPIT THAT OUT, I SAID!" he yelled
again.

And so then I spit the cherry Life Saver on the ground. 'Cause the guy was scaring me, that's why.

Janitor bended down next to me.

"I didn't mean to frighten you, sis," he said. "But I spotted a bunch of dirty candy in the grass. And I was going to clean it up when I finished painting."

He looked serious at me. "Don't you ever eat anything you find on the ground. Do you hear? Not *ever*."

"But I blowed off the germs," I told him.

Janitor shook his head. "You can't blow germs off," he said. "Eating things that you find on the ground is very, very dangerous."

Then Janitor picked up the dangerous candy. "Now run along and play," he said.

I did a big sigh. "Yeah, only I can't," I said.

"'Cause I shot off my big fat mouth in kindergarten. And then I got punishment. And now I hate my bestest friend Lucille."

Janitor smiled a little bit sad. "Life is hard sometimes, isn't it, sis?" he said.

I bobbed my head up and down. "Yes," I said. "Life is P.U."

Then Janitor patted my head and he walked away.

And so guess what?

I just like Janitor.

And that's all.

2
The Cop and
Dr. Smiley

When we came in from recess, Mrs. was clapping her loud hands together again.

"Boys and girls, please take your seats quickly! I've got a wonderful surprise for you!"

Then I got very excited inside my stomach! Because surprises are my most favorite things in the whole world!

"IS IT JELLY DOUGHNUTS?" I shouted.

Mrs. put her finger to her lips. That means *be quiet*.

"YEAH, ONLY GUESS WHAT? JELLY DOUGHNUTS ARE MY MOST FAVORITE KIND OF DOUGHNUTS! EXCEPT I ALSO LIKE THE CREAMY KIND. AND THE CHOCOLATE KIND! AND THE KIND WITH RAINBOW SPRINKLES ON THE TOP!"

After that, my mouth got very watering. And some drool fell on the table.

I wiped it up with my sweater sleeve.

Just then there was a knock on the door.

Mrs. hurried to open it.

"HEY! IT'S A COP!" I hollered very excited.

The cop came into Room Nine.

He had on a blue shirt with a shiny badge. And shiny black boots. And a shiny white motorcycle helmet.

Mrs. smiled. "Boys and girls, I would like you to meet my friend, Officer Mike. Officer Mike is a policeman. Who can tell me what policemen do?"

"I can!" I called out. "They rest people! 'Cause one time some cops rested a guy on my street. And so that means they made him take a nap, I think."

Just then that Jim I hate laughed very loud.

"They didn't *rest* him, stupid!" he hollered. "They *arrested* him! That means they took him to jail. And so your neighbor's a dirty rotten jailbird!"

Then the other kids laughed too. And so I hided my head.

"Yeah, only I hardly even know the guy," I said to just myself.

After that, Officer Mike took off his shiny white helmet. And he told us some other stuff that cops do. Like give our dads speeding tickets. And rest drunk guys.

Also he let us play with his handcuffs and his shiny white helmet. Except for the helmet was very too big for my head. And it covered my whole entire eyes.

"HEY! WHO TURNED OUT THE LIGHTS?" I said.

'Cause that was a funny joke, of course.

Then another knock came at the door.

This time it was a lady in a long white jacket. She was carrying a giant red toothbrush.

"Boys and girls, this is Dr. Smiley," said Mrs. "Dr. Smiley is a children's dentist."

Dr. Smiley hung up some posters of teeth. Then she talked all about Mr. Tooth Decay. And she said to brush our teeth at night. And also in the morning.

"Yeah, 'cause if you don't brush in the morning, your breath smells like stink," I said.

After that I showed Dr. Smiley my wiggling tooth.

"Losing baby teeth is exciting, isn't it?" she asked.

"Yes," I said. "Except for I don't like the part where you cry and spit blood."

Dr. Smiley made a sick face. Then she passed out minty green dental floss. And all the kids in Room Nine practiced flossing.

Flossing is when you pull strings through your mouth.

Only pretty soon an accident happened.

That's because a boy named William winded his floss too tight. And his teeth and head got in a tangled knot ball. And Dr. Smiley couldn't undo him.

Then Mrs. had to call Janitor speedy quick. And so he runned to Room Nine. And he shined his giant flashlight in William's mouth.

And then Dr. Smiley got the dangerous floss right out of there!

Room Nine clapped and clapped.

Dr. Smiley did a bow.

Then Mrs. said that maybe some of us might like to dress up like dentists or police officers on Job Day.

"Yeah, only what if you don't like drunk guys or bloody teeth?" I asked.

Mrs. rolled her eyes way up at the ceiling. Then she walked Officer Mike and Dr. Smiley out into the hall.

That's when Room Nine started buzzing very loud.

Buzzing is what you do when your teacher leaves the room.

"I'm going to dress up like an actress on Job Day," said a girl named Emily.

"I'm going to dress up like a princess," said my bestest friend Lucille that I hate.

I did a giggle. "I'm going to dress up like a bullfighter!" I said.

Then I ran speedy fast around the room. And I butted that mean Jim in the stomach with my head.

And guess what?

I didn't even get caught!

That's what!

3
Me and My
Big Fat Mouth

After school was over, me and my bestest friend named Grace walked to the bus together.

Except for that Grace kept on wanting to skip. And I didn't.

"How come you don't want to skip?" she said. "Me and you always skip to the bus."

"I know, Grace," I said. "But today I've got a very big problem inside my head. And it's called I still don't know what job I want to be when I grow up."

"I do," said that Grace. "I'm going to be Mickey Mouse at Disneyland."

I did a big sigh at her. "Yeah, only too bad for you, Grace," I said. "'Cause there's only one real alive Mickey Mouse. And you're not him."

That Grace laughed very hard.

"Mickey isn't *real*, silly. He's just a mouse suit with a guy inside," she said.

And so just then I felt very sickish inside of my stomach.

'Cause I didn't know Mickey was a suit, that's why.

"What did you have to tell me that for, Grace?" I said real upset. "Now I feel very depressed."

Then I hurried up on the bus. And I scooted way over by the window.

Except I couldn't get any peace and quiet. 'Cause everybody kept on talking about dumb old Job Day.

"I'm going to be a famous singer," said a girl named Rose.

"I'm going to be a famous baton twirler," said another girl named Lynnie.

Then a girl named Charlotte said she was going to be a famous painter. "Famous painters are called artists," she explained. "And artists are very rich."

After that I felt a little bit cheerier. 'Cause guess what? Grandma Miller says I paint beautifully, that's what.

"Hey. Maybe I'll be a famous painter too," I said.

"I'm gonna be a prison guard," said a boy named Roger. "My uncle Roy is a prison guard. And he gets to carry the keys for the whole entire prison."

Then my mouth did a smile. 'Cause one time my dad gave me the key to the front door. And I unlocked it all by myself. And I didn't even need any help!

"Hey. Maybe I might carry keys too, Roger," I said. "'Cause I know how to use those things very good."

Just then William raised his hand very bashful. "I'm going to be a superhero and save people from danger," he said.

And so then I jumped right out of my seat! 'Cause that was the bestest idea of all!

"Me too, William!" I hollered. "'Cause that sounds very exciting, I think. And so I'm going to save people from danger too!"

Then that mean Jim jumped up at me. "Copycat! Copycat! You're just copying everybody else. And anyway, you can't be three jobs! You can only be one!"

I made a growly face at him.

"I *am* just being one job!" I said very

angry. "It's a special kind of job where you paint and you unlock stuff and you save people! So there! Ha-ha on you!"

That Jim made a cuckoo sign at me.

"Goonie," he said. "Goonie B. Jones. There's no such job like that in the whole entire universe!"

"YES, THERE IS! THERE IS TOO,

YOU BIG FAT JIM!" I yelled. "AND IT'S THE BESTEST JOB IN THE WHOLE WIDE WORLD!"

He crossed his arms and did a mean smile.

"Okay. Then what's the name of it?" he said.

Then the bus got very quiet.

And everybody kept on waiting and waiting for me to say the name of my job.

Except for I just couldn't think of anything.

And so my face got very reddish and hottish.

And I felt like P.U. again.

"See? Told ja!" said that mean Jim. "There is no such job! Told ja! Told ja! Told ja!"

After that I sat down very quiet. And I stared out the window.

'Cause the sickish feeling was back inside my stomach again, that's why.

Me and my big fat mouth.

4

Dumb Ollie

I got off the bus at my corner. Then I runned to my house speedy quick.

"HELP! HELP! I'M IN BIG TROUBLE!" I yelled to Mother. "'CAUSE I ACCIDENTALLY SHOT OFF MY BIG FAT MOUTH ON THE BUS! AND NOW I HAVE TO PAINT AND UNLOCK STUFF AND SAVE PEOPLE FROM DANGER! ONLY WHAT KIND OF STUPID DUMB JOB IS THAT?"

"Back here," called Mother.

Back here means the nursery. The nursery is the place where my new baby brother named Ollie lives.

I ran there my very fastest.

Mother was rocking Ollie in the rocking chair. He was a little bit sleeping.

"I NEED TO TALK TO YOU VERY BAD!" I shouted some more. "'CAUSE I DID A BIG FIB. AND NOW I DON'T KNOW HOW TO GET OUT OF IT!"

Just then Ollie woke up. He started crying very much.

"Great," said Mother very growly.

"Yeah, only sorry, but I'm upset here," I explained.

Ollie screeched louder and louder. His voice sounded like a scratchy sore throat.

Mother put him on her lap. Then she

rubbed the sides of her forehead with her fingers.

That's 'cause she had a mybrain headache, I think.

"You're just going to have to wait until I get the baby settled again," she said, still grumpy.

"Yeah, only I can't wait, 'cause—"

Mother butted in. "Not now, Junie B.! I'll be out to talk to you as soon as I can! Now please go!"

Then she pointed at the door.

Pointing means O-U-T.

"Darn it," I said. "Darn it, darn it, darn it."

'Cause that dumb old baby takes up all of Mother's time.

And he's not even interesting.

He doesn't know how to roll over. Or sit up. Or play Chinese checkers.

He is a dud, I think.

I would like to take him back to the hospital. But Mother said no.

After I left the nursery, I went outside in my front yard.

Then I sat in the grass all by myself. And I played with a stick and another ant.

Only this stupid ant bited me. And so I had to drop a rock on his head.

Finally my daddy's car came into the driveway. And my heart got very happy.

"Daddy's home! Daddy's home! Hurray! Hurray!" I yelled.

Then I ran to him. And he picked me up. And I gave him my most biggest hug.

"I'm very glad to see you!" I said. "'Cause

on Monday I have to dress up like what job I want to be. Except for I accidentally said I'm going to paint and save people and carry lots of keys. Only what kind of dumb bunny job is that?"

My daddy put me down. His eyebrows looked confused at me.

"Can we talk about this at dinner?" he asked.

"No," I said. "We have to talk right now. 'Cause I've already waited all I can. And I'm getting tension in me."

"Well, I'm afraid you're just going to have to wait a little while longer," said Daddy. "Because right now I've got to see if your mother needs help with the baby."

Then he did a kiss on my head. And he walked right into the house!

And guess what?

Sometimes I wish stupid dumb Ollie never even came to live with us.

5

Shining

When I went back inside, Ollie was still very screaming.

That's 'cause Mother couldn't find his pacifier.

Pacifiers are what babies like to suck on. Except I don't know why. 'Cause one time I sucked on Ollie's. And it tasted like my red sneakers.

Just then Mother runned out of Ollie's room.

And her hair was very sticking out.

And her clothes were all wrinkly.

And she was wearing one sock, and that's all.

"WHERE IS IT? WHERE IS THE PACI- FIER? IT JUST DIDN'T DISAPPEAR INTO THIN AIR, YOU KNOW!" she hollered very loud.

Then me and Daddy had to help Mother look for the pacifier speedy quick. 'Cause she was losing her grip, I think.

I looked in the couch. That's because sometimes if you push your hand way under the cushions, you can find some good stuff under there.

This time I found three Cheetos and a popcorn.

They were very delicious.

After that, I looked under Daddy's big chair. Only it was too dark to see under there. And so I runned to get the flashlight. 'Cause I learned about flashlights in school, remember?

Flashlights are fun to shine in the dark. I shined it in the dark closet. And also down the dark basement steps.

Then I remembered another dark place. And its name was screaming Ollie's room. 'Cause his shades were pulled down for his nap, that's why.

I runned right there very fast.

"Look," I said to screaming Ollie. "I've got a flashlight."

I shined it on his ceiling.

"See? See that little round circle of shine up there?" I said.

Then I shined it on his jungle wallpaper.

"And see the monkeys, Ollie? And the hippo-pot-of-something?" I asked him.

Only screaming Ollie just kept right on screaming. And he didn't show courtesy to me.

Courtesy is the school word for listening very polite.

That's how come I shined it right in his big fat crying mouth.

Except for just then a problem happened. And it's called Mother sneaked up on me in her quiet sock.

"JUNIE B. JONES! WHAT IN THE WORLD DO YOU THINK YOU'RE DOING?" she hollered.

I did a gulp. Then my heart got very pumpy. Because I was in big trouble, that's why.

"I'm shinin'," I said real soft.

"OUT!" she said. "OUT RIGHT NOW!"

And so that's how come I started to leave. Except for then the flashlight shined on the floor. And I saw something very wonderful down there.

"HEY! LOOK! IT'S THE PACIFIER!" I shouted. "I FOUND THE PACIFIER! IT WAS HIDING UNDER THE ROCKING CHAIR!"

Then I hurried to pick it up. And I gave it to Mother.

Her face got relief on it.

"Thank goodness," she said.

"Yes. Thank goodness," I said back.

Mother wiped the pacifier off. Then she blowed on it very hard.

"Yeah, only you can't blow germs off,

you know," I said. "'Cause stuff that's been on the ground is very dangerous."

And so then Mother gave me the pacifier. And I washed it off with soap and water.

And guess what? Then I put it right in Ollie's mouth. And he stopped crying!

Mother looked proud of me.

"Where did you get so smart?" she asked.

"At school, that's where," I said.

Then all of a sudden my eyes got big and wide. 'Cause a very great idea popped right inside of my head!

"HEY! I THOUGHT OF IT!" I hollered. "I THOUGHT OF WHAT I CAN BE FOR JOB DAY!"

Then I jumped up and down. And I runned down the hall.

Daddy was in his chair reading the paper.

I busted through it with my head.

"I THOUGHT OF IT! I THOUGHT OF WHAT KIND OF JOB I CAN BE WHEN I GROW UP!"

Daddy said, "Slow down," to me. That's because he didn't know what the heck I was talking about, of course.

"Yeah, only I can't slow down," I explained. "'Cause I'm very celebrating! And now I don't have tension in me anymore!"

Just then Mother came into the room.

"What's all the excitement about?" she said.

I clapped my hands together. "I have a 'nouncement, that's what it's all about!" I said real happy.

"Well, what is it?" said Mother. "Tell us!"

And so then I stood up straight and tall.

And I told Mother and Daddy the name of the job I'm going to be when I grow up!

"That's a good one, right?" I said very excited. "That's the bestest job you ever heard of, isn't it?"

Except for Mother and Daddy didn't answer me. They just kept on looking and looking at each other.

Then Daddy did a funny smile.

And Mother said the word *ho boy*.

6
Tingling

I couldn't sleep for the whole weekend. That's because I had tingling excitement in me about Job Day. And my brain wouldn't settle down.

And so on Monday, I zoomed to the bus stop very fast.

"Look, Mr. Woo!" I said to my bus driver. "Look what I'm wearing today!"

Then I opened my jacket and I showed him my job clothes.

"See? It's nice pants. And dangling keys. And a paintbrush," I said. "Except for I can't

tell you what I am, 'cause it's my special
secret."

Then I plopped down in my seat. And me
and Mr. Woo drove to the next corner.

That's where my bestest friend Grace got
on.

She was wearing Mickey Mouse ears and
a dress with red and white polka dotties on
it!

"Grace!" I said very smiling. "You look
very beautiful in that dotty thing."

"I know it," she said. "That's because I
changed my mind about who I'm going to
be when I grow up. Now I'm going to be
Minnie instead of Mickey."

Then I stopped smiling. And my stomach
felt very sickish inside again.

'Cause that meant Minnie Mouse was a
fake too.

"Disneyland is a fib," I said.

After that, the bus stopped again. And William got on.

He was wearing a Superman outfit. Except he had a W on the front of him. And not the letter S.

"The W stands for William," he said to Mr. Woo.

"Does that mean you can fly?" asked Mr. Woo.

Then William grinned very big. And he held out his arms. And he jumped way high in the air.

Except for he didn't fly.

And so he just sat down.

After that, other kids got on the bus, too.

And Roger had on keys just like me. And also plastic handcuffs.

And Charlotte was wearing a red paint apron with some watercolors in the pocket.

And that mean Jim was wearing a white bathrobe.

"Hey! I've got a bathrobe just like that, Jim!" I said very friendly.

"It's not a bathrobe, dummy," he said. "I'm a kung fu karate guy."

"Jim is a kung fu karate guy," I said to Grace. "Except for he just got out of the bathtub."

Then me and her laughed and laughed. 'Cause that was a funny joke, of course.

And Job Day was going to be the funnest day in the whole wide world!

7
Jobs and Jobs

When I got off the bus, I zoomed to Room Nine. That's because I wanted Job Day to start very quick.

Only first we had to take attendance.

And then we had to say *I pledge allegiance to the flag of the United States of America, and to the republic for which it stands.*

Except I don't know what that dumb story is even talking about.

Then finally Mrs. clapped her loud hands together.

And guess what? Job Day started, that's what!

"Boys and girls, you all look wonderful in your outfits!" Mrs. said. "I can't wait to learn what all of you want to be when you grow up! Who would like to go first?"

"I WOULD! I WOULD!" I yelled out.

Only then my bestest friend Lucille raised her hand very polite. And she got to go first.

Lucille looked the most beautifulest I've ever seen her.

She was wearing a new dress that her nanna bought for her. It was the color of pink velvet.

Also she had on shiny pink shoes. And socks with bows and lace on them.

Lucille's nanna is loaded, I think.

Lucille went to the front of the room. She reached into a little bag and pulled out a sparkling crown with jewels on it!

Then all of Room Nine said, "Ooooh."

Except for not the boys.

"When I grow up, I'm going to marry a prince," she said. "And I'll be a princess. And my name will be Princess Lucille."

Then she put the sparkling crown on her head. And she looked like a fairy tale guy.

Mrs. smiled. "That's a lovely thought, Lucille," she said.

"I know," said Lucille. "My nanna says if you marry a prince, you're set for life."

After that, Lucille said her dress costed eighty-five. And her shoes costed forty-five. And her lacy socks costed six fifty plus tax.

Then Mrs. told Lucille to sit down.

Ricardo went next.

He was wearing a round yellow hat. It was the kind of hat you can bang on.

"This is called a hard hat," he said. "You have to wear it when you're building tall buildings. Or else somebody might drop a hammer from way up high. And it could hit you on the head and kill you."

Mrs. smiled. "So you're interested in construction, right, Ricardo?" she asked.

But Ricardo just kept on talking about other stuff that could fall on your head and kill you. Like a paint can. And an electric drill. And a lunchbox.

Then Mrs. said, "Sit down," to him, too.

That's when William raised his hand. Only he was being very bashful. And he wouldn't go to the front of the room.

"You don't have to be nervous, William," said Mrs. "Just tell us what you want to be when you grow up."

William covered his face with his hands.

"Super William," he said very quiet.

Then he got out of his seat. And he jumped way high in the air. Only his cape got tangled up in his chair. And he crashed into the table.

After that, Super William got very sniffling. And Mrs. said we would get back to him later.

Then lots of other kids talked about their jobs.

Like a boy named Clifton is going to be a rich and famous astronaut.

And a girl named Lily is going to be a rich and famous movie star. And also she wants to direct.

And a boy named Ham is going to be a rich and famous boss of a big company. And he taught us how to say the word *you're fired*.

And here's the bestest one of all! 'Cause a boy named Jamal Hall is going to be the rich and famous president of the whole United States!

"Cool!" said Ricardo.

Then the other boys said, "Cool," too.

I did a secret smile. Yeah, only not as cool as my job, I thought to just myself.

Then I raised my hand very polite. And Mrs. called my name.

"OH, BOY!" I shouted. "OH, BOY! OH, BOY! 'CAUSE MINE IS EVEN BETTER THAN PRESIDENT OF THE UNITED STATES!"

I zoomed speedy quick to the front of the room.

Then my excitement wouldn't stay inside of me anymore.

"A JANITOR! I'M GOING TO BE A JANITOR!" I hollered out.

After that, I jingled my jangly keys! And I waved my paintbrush in the air! And I clapped and clapped!

Only too bad for me.

'Cause nobody clapped back.

And here's something even worser.

Room Nine started laughing very much. And it was the mean kind.

"SHE WANTS TO BE A JANITOR!" they yelled.

Then they pointed at my brown pants.

And they called me the name of stupid.

And I didn't know what to do. 'Cause I felt very crumbling inside.

And so I just kept on standing there and standing there.

And my eyes got a little bit of wet in them. And my nose started running very much.

That's how come I covered my face up.

"They're not having courtesy for me," I said real soft.

Only just then Mrs. clapped her angry hands together. And she scolded Room Nine a real lot.

"Junie B. is right," she said. "Being a janitor is a very important job. You have to be hardworking and reliable and very, very trustworthy."

I peeked through my fingers at her.

"Yeah, and don't forget the part where you have to save people from danger," I said.

Then that Jim I hate laughed right out loud. "Janitors don't save people from danger, you goonie bird!" he said.

I stamped my foot at him. "Yes, they do! They do too! Because one time I was eating a dangerous Life Saver. And Janitor made me spit it out! And also he brought his flashlight to Room Nine. And he saved William from the dangerous dental floss!"

Then I held up my jingling keys.

"And see these things? Keys are what Janitor unlocks the bathroom door with. Or else we couldn't even go to the toilet!"

Then I showed him my paintbrush.

"And Janitor paints litter cans, too," I said. "And painting is the funnest thing I love!"

That Jim did a mean smile. "Yeah, well, too bad for you, but you're a girl. And janitors have to be boys. So there."

I runned to his table. "No, they do not,

you stupid head Jim!" I said. "Girls can be anything boys can be! Right, Mrs.? Right? Right? 'Cause I saw that on *Sesame Street*. And also on *Oprah*."

Mrs. did a smile.

Then my bestest friend Grace started to clap.

And guess what? All of the other girls in Room Nine clapped too.

8
Gus Vallony

Today Janitor came to Room Nine for Show and Tell!

And it was the funnest day I ever saw!

That's 'cause he brought his very big tool-box with him.

And we played a game called Name the Tools.

And guess what?

I knew the saw.

And the hammer.

And the metric socket set with adjustable ratchet.

Then Janitor showed us how to use his stuff.

And Charlotte got to shine his giant flashlight.

And my bestest friend Grace got to push his big broom.

And lucky duck Lucille got to clean the chalkboard with his squishy sponge.

Except for then a little bit of trouble happened. 'Cause I wanted the mop. Only that stupid head Jim wouldn't let go of it. And so I had to pinch his arm.

After that, the mop got removed from us.

Removed is the school word for snatched right out of our hands.

After that, Janitor sat in a chair. And Room Nine sat all around him.

Then he told us all about himself and his job.

And guess what?

He's been Janitor for fourteen years.

And he was borned in a different country from ours.

And his name is Gus Vallony!

"Hey! I love that name of Gus Vallony!" I hollered out. "'Cause Vallony is my favorite kind of sandwich!"

Then I smiled very proud.

"And guess what else?" I said to Room Nine. "Me and Janitor are bestest friends. And sometimes he calls me the nickname of sis!"

Then Janitor winked at me.

And so I winked back. Except for both my eyes kept on shutting. And so I had to hold one of them open with my fingers.

"I really like that Gus Vallony," I whispered to my bestest friend Lucille.

Only then that dumb girl named Lily heard what I said.

And she started singing, *"Junie B.'s got a boyyy friennnd. Junie B.'s got a boyyy friennnd."*

And so that's how come I felt very embarrassed.

"Me and my big fat mouth!" I said.

Then Mrs. laughed.

And Janitor laughed.

And everybody else laughed too.

After that, Janitor had to go back to work. And so Mrs. shook his hand.

Then Room Nine clapped and clapped for him.

And Janitor smiled.

And his jingly keys jangled all the way out the door.

BARBARA PARK

junie b. jones®

Is a Party Animal

illustrated by
Denise Brunkus

Contents

1. The Richiest Nanna   75

2. Excellent Work of Us   82

3. The Rules   90

4. Packing My Bags   96

5. Going to the Ball   105

6. Bouncing   118

7. Peeping   135

8. Morning   138

1

The Richiest Nanna

My name is Junie B. Jones. The B stands for Beatrice. Except I don't like Beatrice. I just like B and that's all.

I am almost six years old.

Almost six is when you ride the bus to afternoon kindergarten.

My bestest friend named Grace rides the bus with me.

Every day she sits right exactly next to me. 'Cause I save her a seat, that's why.

Saving a seat is when you zoom on the bus. And you hurry up and sit down. And then you quick put your feet on the seat next to you.

After that, you keep on screaming the word "SAVED! SAVED! SAVED!" And no one even sits next to you. 'Cause who wants to sit next to a screamer? That's what I would like to know.

Me and that Grace have another bestest friend at school. Her name is Lucille.

Lucille does not ride the bus with us. Her richie nanna drives her to school in a big gold car. It is called a Cattle Act, I think.

And guess what?

Today that big gold Cattle Act was driving right next to the school bus!

I banged on my window very excited.

"LUCILLE! HEY, LUCILLE! IT'S ME! IT'S JUNIE B. JONES! I AM RIGHT NEXT TO YOU ON THE SCHOOL BUS!

SEE ME? SEE ME, LUCILLE? I AM BANGING ON MY WINDOW VERY EXCITED!"

Lucille did not see me.

"YEAH, ONLY HERE'S THE PROBLEM! YOUR NANNA JUST SPEEDED UP HER CAR. AND NOW YOU ARE ZOOMING WAY AHEAD OF THE BUS. AND SO HOW COME I AM STILL SHOUTING AT YOU? THAT'S WHAT I WOULD LIKE TO KNOW."

I sat down and smoothed my skirt.

"Lucille's nanna has a lead foot, apparently," I said to that Grace.

"Lucille's nanna is rich," she said back.

"Lucille's nanna is very, *very* rich," I said. "She owns a big, giant house with a million rooms in it. And she lets Lucille's whole entire family live there. 'Cause it is

77

way too big for just one nanna."

"Wow," said that Grace.

"I know it is wow, Grace," I said. "My nanna just owns a plain, old, regular house, and that's it."

That Grace did a sad sigh.

"My nanna just owns a condo in Florida," she said.

Then me and that Grace looked at each other very glum.

"Our nannas are losers," I said.

After that, we didn't talk the rest of the trip.

Only guess what?

When we got to school, we saw the nanna's big gold car! It was parked right in the parking lot!

Me and that Grace runned there speedy fast.

"Lucille! Lucille! It's me! It's Junie B. Jones! Plus also it's that Grace! We are running to see your richie nanna!"

We opened the door and sticked our heads inside.

"Hi, Nanna!" I said.

"Hello, Nanna!" said that Grace.

The nanna looked surprised at us.

"Yeah, only you don't even have to be afraid of us," I said. "'Cause we know your grandgirl very good. Plus we won't even harm you."

Me and that Grace got in the back.

I rubbed my hand on the seat.

"Oooo! I love this rich velvety interior," I told her.

I put my cheek on it.

"These seats are ooo-la-la, Nanna," I said.

Lucille looked grouchy at me. "Don't call her *nanna!* She's *my* nanna! Not *your* nanna!"

"Lucille!" said the nanna very shocked. "What's gotten into you? Your little friends are darling."

"Yes, Lucille," I said. "I am darling. Plus that Grace is darling. And so, back off. Right, Nanna?"

The nanna did a loud hoot of laughing.

"Hey! You are the friendliest nanna I ever saw!" I said. "And so maybe me and Grace can come see your richie house sometime."

Lucille's nanna did another loud hoot.

Then me and that Grace did loud hoots, too. And all of us kept on laughing and laughing.

Only not Lucille.

2
Excellent Work of Us

Lucille sits at my same table in Room Nine.

She kept on being mad at me. Only I don't even know why.

"That is a lovely sweater you are wearing today, Lucille," I said very pleasant.

She scooted her chair away from me.

I scooted next to her.

"Oooo. Is that sequins I see on the collar? 'Cause sequins are my favorite little, shiny, roundish beady things," I told her.

I touched one of the sequins.

Lucille pushed my hand away.

I tickled her under the chin very friendly.

"Coochie-coochie-coo," I said real fun.

Lucille turned her back to me.

I swinged her ponytail.

"Swingy, swingy, swingy," I sang.

Just then, Lucille springed out of her chair.

"STOP TOUCHING ME!" she hollered right in my face.

My teacher hurried to my table speedy fast.

Her name is Mrs.

She has another name, too. But I just like Mrs. and that's all.

I smiled at her very cute.

"Hello. How are you today? Me and Lucille are not even fighting. We are just having a loudish conservation."

Mrs. looked funny at me.

"I think you mean *conversation*, Junie B.," she said. "*Conservation* is when people save something."

I tapped on my chin very thinking.

Then all of a sudden, I jumped up real excited.

"Yeah, only I *do*, Mrs.! I *do* save something!" I said. "I save that Grace a seat on the bus!"

I shouted across the room. "GRACE! HEY, GRACE! TELL MRS. HOW I SAVE YOU A SEAT ON THE BUS! 'CAUSE SHE THINKS I DON'T KNOW MY WORDS, APPARENTLY!"

That Grace shouted back. "SHE DOES, TEACHER! JUNIE B. SAVES ME A SEAT ON THE BUS EVERY SINGLE DAY!"

I smiled very proud. "See, Mrs.? I told

you! I told you I save something!"

Mrs. stared at me a real long time.

Then she closed her eyes.

And she said she needs a vacation.

Pretty soon, the bell rang for recess.

Lucille didn't even wait for me and Grace. She runned right out the door without us.

That is how come we had to chase that girl down and surround her.

I made my voice very growly.

"I am at the end of my string with you, madam!" I said. "How come you keep being mad at us? 'Cause me and Grace didn't even do anything to you!"

Lucille stamped her foot.

"Yes, you did! You ruined everything! I was begging my nanna for a little white poodle! And she was almost going to say yes! And then you guys got in my back seat! And now everything is ruined!"

I did a huffy breath at her.

"Yeah, only that is not even our fault, Lucille! 'Cause we didn't know you were begging! We just wanted to see your richie nanna, and that's all!"

"I don't care!" said Lucille. "You should have stayed away! You guys have your *own* nannas!"

Just then, me and that Grace got very glum again.

"I *know* we have nannas, Lucille," I said. "But they are not *richie* nannas like yours."

That Grace hanged her head.

"Our nannas are just *regular* nannas," she said.

"They are duds," I said real soft.

After that, Lucille acted nicer to us.

"Sorry," she said. "Sorry about your regular nannas. I was just upset about not getting my poodle, that's all. Usually my nanna gives me whatever I want."

Just then, I smiled real big. 'Cause a great idea popped in my head, that's why! It came right out of thin hair!

"Lucille! Hey, Lucille! Maybe me and Grace can come to your nanna's house! And we can help you beg for a poodle!"

I danced all around.

"And here is *another* great idea! Maybe we can even spend the night, possibly! 'Cause me and Grace never even saw a richie house before! Plus that way we can beg for your poodle the whole entire evening!"

All of a sudden, that Grace started dancing all around, too. "When can we come? When can we come?" she asked.

I clapped my hands very thrilled.

"I am available on Saturday, I believe!" I said.

"Me, too! I am available on Saturday, too!" said that Grace.

Lucille thought and thought.

"Hmm. I don't know about Saturday," she said. "My mommy and daddy and brother are going away for the weekend. So it's just going to be my nanna and me."

I jumped up and down.

"Hurray!" I said. "That will work out even better! 'Cause now we can beg your nanna with positively no interruptions!"

Just then, Lucille started to smile.

"Hey, yeah! Why didn't *I* think of that?" she said.

I pointed at myself.

"'Cause I'm the brains of this outfit, that's why!" I said real happy.

After that, all of us skipped around and around.

Plus me and that Grace did a high five.

'CAUSE WE WERE ON OUR WAY TO THE NANNA'S, OF COURSE!!!

3
The Rules

Guess what!!?! Guess what!!?!

On Friday, Lucille's nanna called my mother!

And she invited me to spend the night with Lucille on Saturday!

And Mother didn't even say no!

My feet zoomed all around the house when I heard that!

"I'M SPENDIN' THE NIGHT! I'M SPENDIN' THE NIGHT! I'M SPENDIN' THE NIGHT!" I shouted.

I zoomed into my baby brother Ollie's room.

"HEY, OLLIE! I'M SPENDIN' THE NIGHT! I'M SPENDIN' THE NIGHT! I'M SPENDIN' THE—"

Just then, Mother runned in the door and she swished me right out of there.

It was not pleasant.

I brushed myself off.

"Yeah, only you shouldn't actually swish people," I said kind of quiet.

Mother raised her voice at me.

"How many times, Junie B.? How many times have I told you to stay out of Ollie's room while he's sleeping? Huh? How many?"

I thinked for a minute.

"A million bazillion," I said. "But that is just a ballpark figure."

Mother glared at me very mad.

I rocked back and forth on my feet.

"A ballpark figure is when you don't know the actual figure. And so you make up a figure. 'Cause that will get people off your back," I explained. "My boyfriend named Ricardo told me that. His father sells insurance, I believe."

Mother tapped her angry foot.

"We are *not* talking about Ricardo's father, Junie B. We are talking about going into Ollie's room while he's sleeping. And besides, I haven't said that you could spend the night at Lucille's. I want to talk it over with your father first."

I hugged her leg.

"Please, Mother? Please? Please? I'll be good. I promise, I promise, I—"

Just then, the front door opened.

It was my Daddy!

He was home from work!

I runned to him like a speedy rocket.

Then I hugged his leg, too. And he couldn't even shake me off.

"I'll be good, Daddy! I promise! I promise! I promise!"

All of a sudden, Mother swished me away again. She put me down in the living room.

Then she and Daddy did whispering in the hall.

And guess what?

They said I could go to Lucille's!!!

"YIPPEE! YIPPEE! YIPPEE!" I shouted.

After that, I started to zoom some more. But Daddy quick grabbed me by my belt.

"Yeah, only here's the problem. I'm not actually zooming," I told him.

"No...*here's* the problem," said Daddy. "Before you spend the night with Lucille, you have to agree to the rules."

I raised up my eyebrows.

"Rules?" I asked. "There's rules involved?"

"*Lots* of rules," said Daddy.

Then he and Mother bended down next to me. And they told me the rules of spending the night.

They are: *No running, no jumping, no shouting, no squealing, no hollering, no snooping, no spying, no arguing, no fighting, no cheating at games, no talking back to the nanna, no breaking other people's toys, no grumping, no crying, no fibbing, no tickling people when they say no, no staying up late, and absolutely no head-butting.*

After I heard the rules, I did a sigh.

"Yeah, only that doesn't actually leave me much to work with," I said.

Mother ruffled my hair.

"Sorry, kiddo. But that's the deal," she said. "Take it or leave it."

"Take it!" I shouted out. "I'll take the deal!"

Then I kissed Mother and Daddy on their cheeks.

And I hugged them very tight.

And they couldn't shake me off again.

4
Packing My Bags

The next morning was Saturday.

I jumped out of bed and runned to the kitchen.

Then I got a big, giant plastic bag. And I runned back to my room to pack for Lucille's.

First, I packed my favorite pillow. Then I packed my pajamas and my bathrobe and my slippers that look like bunnies. Also, I packed my blanket and my sheets and a small, attractive throw rug.

Finally, I packed my stuffed elephant named Philip Johnny Bob.

He looked up at me from inside the bag. *Yeah, only here's the problem,* he said. *You're not actually supposed to put me in a plastic bag. 'Cause I could suffercate in this thing.*

My eyes got big and wide.

"Oh no!" I said real upset. "I forgot about that!"

That's how come I quick got my scissors and cut air holes for that guy.

Philip Johnny Bob sniffed the air. *Better,* he said.

I petted his trunk. Then I went into the family room. And I watched cartoons till Mother got up.

Pretty soon, I heard her slippers in the hall.

"MOTHER! MOTHER! I'M ALL READY!" I said. "I'M ALL READY TO GO TO LUCILLE'S!"

I pulled Mother into my room and showed her my plastic bag.

Mother shook her head. "Waaaay too much stuff," she said.

Then she got a teeny suitcase from the shelf. And she packed my pajamas and my slippers and my robe and my toothbrush.

After that, she got a sleeping bag from her closet. And she put my pillow on top of it.

"There. That's all you'll need. You're all set," she said.

I springed into the air.

"ALL SET!" I hollered real joyful. "JUNIE B. JONES IS ALL SET FOR LUCILLE'S!"

After that, I quick grabbed Philip Johnny Bob. And I dragged my stuff to the front door.

"ALL RIGHTIE! LET'S BE ON OUR WAY!" I shouted very excited.

Mother was in baby Ollie's room. She didn't come.

"OKIE DOKE! I'M GOING OUTSIDE NOW! JUNIE B. JONES IS GOING OUT-SIDE TO GET IN THE CAR!" I shouted louder.

Just then, Mother runned to get me.

"No, Junie B.! No! I'm not taking you to Lucille's, remember? Lucille's nanna is pick-ing you up at three o'clock. I told you that. I'm *sure* I did."

All of a sudden, my shoulders got very slumping. 'Cause I didn't actually remember that information, that's why.

"Darn it," I said very sad. "Three o'clock takes forever."

After that, I slumped to the table and ate my breakfast.

Then I sat on my front step.

And I swinged on my swings.

And I read some books.

And I ate a cheese sandwich.

And I counted to a million bazillion.

And I sat on my step some more.

And then guess what?

Three o'clock finally came!

I saw the big gold car in my driveway!

"HEY! SHE'S HERE! SHE'S HERE! SHE'S HERE!" I yelled real thrilled.

Mother and Daddy hurried to the door.

"Are you ready to go?" said Mother.

"READY!" I yelled. "JUNIE B. JONES IS READY TO GO!"

The richie nanna got out of her car.

I throwed my arms around her.

"HELLO, NANNA! HELLO! HELLO! I HAVE BEEN WAITING FOR YOU THE WHOLE LIVELONG DAY!"

Mother pulled me off of that woman.

"Sorry," she said. "I'm afraid Junie B. has a little extra energy in her. She's been sitting on the step for hours."

I leaped way high in the air.

"SITTING ON THE STEP!" I said. "JUNIE B. JONES HAS BEEN SITTING ON THE STEP!"

Daddy and Mother carried my things to the big gold Cattle Act.

And guess what? When they opened the door, Lucille and that Grace were already in the backseat!

"LUCILLE! GRACE! I DIDN'T EVEN KNOW YOU WERE ALREADY HERE! AND SO THIS IS A DELIGHTFUL SURPRISE!"

I reached inside to try to tickle them. But Mother pulled my hand away.

"Please, Junie B. Don't start," she said.

I saluted her.

"Aye, aye, Captain," I said real hilarious.

After that, I got in the car and I bounced on the softie seat.

Only too bad for me. 'Cause I accidentally bounced too high. And I banged my head on the roof.

The nanna did a gasp.

I patted her.

"Yeah, only that didn't even faze me," I said.

After that, I buckled up my seat belt.

And I waved good-bye to Mother and Daddy.

And the nanna drove us away.

5
Going to the Ball

Lucille was sitting in the middle.

She whispered real quiet to me and that Grace.

"Beg for my poodle," she said. "You *promised*, remember? You promised to beg for my poodle."

Me and that Grace looked and looked at each other. 'Cause we didn't actually want to do that particular thing.

Lucille poked us.

"Come on! You *promised!*" she whispered. "You promised to beg!"

I did a sigh.

Then I thinked and thinked about what to say.

Finally, I took a deep breath.

"Hey, Nanna. Guess what? Lucille wants a poodle, apparently. And so could you buy her one, do you think?" I asked.

"Yes, could you?" asked that Grace. "'Cause she is making us beg you. Or else we can't spend the night."

The nanna's mouth came all the way open.

"Ohhhh. So *that's* what this is all about, huh? Well, my granddaughter knows perfectly well that I am allergic to dogs. So you can tell Lucille that a poodle is out of the question, I'm afraid."

I patted Lucille very understanding.

"A poodle is out of the question, we're afraid," I said.

Lucille kicked her feet up and down.

"Beg *harder*," she whispered. "You have to beg *harder*."

I did a frown.

"Are you firm on that, Nanna?" I asked.

"No poodle, Lucille!" said the nanna very snappish.

Lucille kicked her feet some more.

"I *knew* that dumb idea wouldn't work!" she grouched.

Just then, the car stopped in front of a big iron gate.

Grace's eyes opened big and wide.

"Wow! This gate looks like a *castle* gate," she said.

Lucille smiled a teeny bit.

"It's not a castle gate, you sillyhead,

Grace," she said. "This is the gate to my *house.*"

The nanna pushed a button, and the gate opened right in front of our eyes.

"Hey, that button is like *magic!*" I said.

Lucille smiled bigger.

After that, the nanna drove down a long driveway. She stopped in front of a big, beautiful house.

Lucille jumped out of the car and ran inside.

Me and that Grace followed after her.

And guess what? Lucille's house was even beautifuller on the *inside* than it was on the *outside!*

There was a beautiful long row of stairs. And a beautiful big bowl of flowers. And a beautiful, giant, sparkly ceiling light made out of glass.

I did a gasp at that glistening thing!

"That light takes my breathing away!" I said.

Lucille skipped all around in a circle.

She singed a loud song in our ears.

"SEE? SEE? I TOLD YOU I WAS RICH! SEE? SEE? I TOLD YOU I WAS RICH!" she sang.

She made that song up, I believe.

After that, she took our hands and showed us all the rooms in her house.

She showed us the living room. And the dining room. And the kitchen. And the big giant patio. And the daddy's office. And the mother's office. And the family room. And the pool room where you play pool. And the outside pool where you swim. And the hot tub. And the library. And the gym. And the nanna's room. And the mother and daddy's room. And the fancy gold bathroom with the Jacuzzi. And the brother's room. And a whole, whole bunch of guest rooms.

Then finally, Lucille showed us her very own bedroom!

And it looked like a bedroom where a princess lived!

Lucille's bed had a pink frilly roof on top of it.

"That is called a *canopy*," she explained. "It matches my pink silk draperies and my pink silk bedspread. And my pink telephone. And my plush pink rug. And my wallpaper with pink flowers in it.

"And see my TV? And my stereo? And my computer? And my CD player?"

She pointed to the corner. "And did you notice all of my big stuffed animals standing over there?" she asked.

My eyes popped out at those giant guys. The giraffe was bigger than me even!

Me and that Grace ran to play with them.

"NO! STOP! DON'T!" shouted Lucille. "YOU'RE NOT ALLOWED TO TOUCH THEM! THEY ARE JUST FOR SHOW!"

"Huh?" said that Grace.

"What?" I said. "How come?"

"Because they were expensive, *that's* how come," she said. "Those animals costed my nanna a fortune."

"Oh," I said kind of disappointed.

"Oh," said that Grace.

We sat down on Lucille's bed.

Lucille shouted at us again. "NO! GET UP! YOU'RE NOT ALLOWED TO SIT THERE! THAT BEDSPREAD IS JUST FOR SHOW!"

Me and that Grace springed right off of there.

Lucille quick smoothed the material with her hand.

"Don't you two know *anything?*" she said. "This bedspread is made out of *silk,* I told you. I'm not allowed to get it soiled."

"Oh," I said.

"Oh," said that Grace.

After that, Lucille skipped over to her dresser. And she pressed a button on her mirror.

A million bazillion lights came on!

"Look at this," she said. "This is my very own professional makeup mirror! It is the same kind of mirror that they use for movie stars. My nanna brought it all the way from Hollywood, California!"

Me and that Grace runned to the sparkly

mirror. We looked at ourselves in the bright
lights.

Then we sticked out our tongues and
made funny faces.

Lucille quick turned it off.

"It is *not* a toy!" she grouched.

After that, me and that Grace just stood

very still. And we didn't touch anything.

"This is going to be a long evening," I said kind of quiet.

Only just then, something very wonderful happened!

Lucille's nanna came in the room! And she was carrying a big box of dress-up clothes!

"I thought you little gals might have fun with some of my old evening gowns," she said real nice. "They're as old as the hills. But they're still quite stunning."

Lucille runned to the box speedy quick.

"Let's play Cinderella!" she said.

She pulled out a beautiful, sparkly pink gown.

"I'M CINDERELLA!" she shouted.

Then that Grace shoved me out of her way. And she runned to the box, too.

She pulled out a sparkly *blue* gown.

"I'M THE FAIRY GODMOTHER!" she yelled.

I did a huffy breath at those two. 'Cause now I had to be the ugly stepsisters, probably.

I bended down and searched through the box very careful.

Then all of a sudden, my hands felt something long and silky and softie.

I quick pulled it out of there.

The nanna's whole face lighted up.

"Oh my goodness! My old feather boa!" she said. "Why, I haven't seen that thing in years!"

I danced all around with that lovely thing.

"I love this, Nanna! I love this old feather boa!"

Just then, another great idea popped in my brain.

"Hey! I know! I will be the famous singer that sings at Cinderella's ball!"

Lucille and Grace looked funny at me.

"What singer?" said Lucille.

"There's no singer," said that Grace.

I stamped my foot at them.

"Yes, there is! There is, too, a singer! And I am her! And my name is Florence the Famous Singer! And I will be performing

show tunes from the hit musical *Annie!* So there!"

Lucille and Grace shrugged their shoulders at me.

Then they dressed up in their beautiful gowns.

And they went to the ball.

And I sang "The Sun Will Come Out Tomorrow."

6
Bouncing

After we finished playing Cinderella, the nanna called us to dinner.

Me and Lucille and that Grace skipped into the big dining room. We sat at a long, shiny table.

Pretty soon, Lucille's nanna came in from the kitchen. And she gave us our dinner.

And guess what?

Its name was beans and Frank!

"Hurray!" I said. "Hurray for beans and

Frank! 'Cause this is my favorite kind of home cooking!"

The nanna did a teeny smile.

"Well, we usually have a cook. But I gave her the night off," she said.

After that, the nanna poured milk into beautiful sparkly glasses.

"Oooo, Nanna! These are your best crystal glasses!" said Lucille real thrilled. "I love these expensive things!"

"Me, too! I love these expensive things, too!" I said.

Only too bad for me. 'Cause nobody even told me that crystal glasses were very heavy.

And so when I picked up my glass, it slipped right out of my hand.

And it fell on the floor!

And it broke into lots of pieces!

Lucille's whole mouth came open.

"OH NO! YOU BROKE IT! YOU BROKE MY NANNA'S CRYSTAL GLASS!"

The nanna's face was reddish and scrunchy.

"Sorry, Nanna," I said real soft. "Sorry I broke your crystal glass."

The nanna sucked her cheeks way into her head.

"Let's just try to be more careful, shall we, dear?" she said.

I bobbed my head up and down.

"We shall," I said back.

After that, I ate my beans and Frank very careful. Only pretty soon, my Frank spilled off my fork. And he landed on the nanna's white tablecloth.

"OH NO!" hollered Lucille. "THAT'S MY NANNA'S GOOD LINEN TABLE-

CLOTH! SHE BROUGHT IT ALL THE WAY FROM IRELAND!"

The nanna's face was twisty and puffy.

I quick pushed my plate away from me.

My stomach felt in a tight knot.

"Yeah, only guess what? I am not actually hungry anymore. And so I will just sit here and not spill anything, I think."

The nanna cleaned up my messes with a wet cloth.

After she finished, she brought us chocolate ice cream for dessert.

Only too bad for me. 'Cause a teeny plop of ice cream dropped right off my spoon. And it landed on my chair cushion.

The nanna did a big breath.

"You're a bit of a bull in a china shop, aren't you, dear?" she said.

"Sorry, Nanna," I said. "Sorry, sorry, sorry."

The nanna patted my hand very stiffish.

"Quite all right," she said kind of mumbly.

After that, I got down from the table. And me and my friends went back to Lucille's room.

And guess what?

Things got funner!

'Cause Lucille said we could play with the games in her closet! On account of they weren't even expensive!

First, we played Chutes and Ladders. Then we played Twister and Bingo and Chinese checkers and Tic-Tac-Toad and Candyland. Plus also we played Let's Spin Till We Get Real Dizzy and Fall Down.

And guess what? I didn't even break anything!

"Hey! I think I am getting the hang of this party!" I said very happy.

Just then, the nanna knocked on Lucille's door.

"Time for you ladies to put your pajamas on," she told us.

I danced all around the room real happy.

"Hurray!" I said "Hurray for pajamas! 'Cause I brought my favorites!"

I quick put them on.

"See them, Nanna? See how biggish and baggish they are? That is how come they feel so comfortable!"

The nanna's eyes looked down at me.

"How very...*charming*," she said.

Just then, that Grace jumped right in front of me.

"Look at mine, Nanna!" she said. "See

mine? My pajamas have neon-green polka dotties on them!"

"How very…*colorful*," said the nanna.

All of a sudden, Lucille popped out of her big closet.

"Ta-da! Look at *me*, everyone! I am wearing my beauteous pink satin nightie! See me? See how lovely I look! I look like a gorgeous model in this thing!" she said.

Lucille let me and that Grace feel her material.

"How very…*smoothie*," I said.

After that, me and Grace unrolled our sleeping bags on the floor. And the nanna took the silk bedspread off Lucille's bed.

"Time to get your beauty sleep, Princess," she told Lucille.

Then those two kissed and hugged good night. And the nanna shut the door.

Only guess what?

Lucille didn't even get in bed. She kept twirling all around in her pink satin night-gown.

"This is how models twirl," she said. "They twirl so you can see their fronts and their backs."

Lucille wouldn't stop twirling.

"See my front? See my back?" she said.

Me and that Grace got up on her bed to watch her twirl.

Lucille's bed was soft and cushy.

We bounced up there a teeny bit.

Lucille stopped twirling.

"Hey! Don't!" she said. "That bed is for beauty sleep *only!*"

I patted her bed very admiring.

"Yeah, only it's too bad we can't actually play up here. 'Cause this mattress is a *bouncy* one," I said.

Just then, Lucille's face did a sneaky smile.

"Want to bounce?" she said real soft.

"Want to really, *really* bounce?"

She tippytoed to her door and looked down the hall.

"Come on," she whispered. "Follow me."

I grabbed Philip Johnny Bob and followed after Lucille and that Grace.

We tippytoed down the hall and around the corner.

Then Lucille opened the door to a big guest room. And there was a giant bed in that place!

"See it!" she said. "See how *huge* that bed is? My nanna had it specially made in case we have tall company!"

Lucille quick shut the door after us.

"Come on! Let's go!" she said.

And so all of us runned to the big bed speedy quick! And we jumped and jumped and jumped on that thing!

I sang a joyful song.

It is called "Jumping, Jumping, Jumping on the Giant Bed."

"JUMPING...JUMPING...JUMPING ON THE GIANT BED," I sang.

Only too bad for me. 'Cause all of a sudden, I remembered something very important. And it is called *Mother and Daddy said no jumping.*

I got off the bed speedy fast.

"Yeah, only here's the problem," I said. "I am not actually allowed to jump. 'Cause Mother and Daddy said *no jumping.* And so you guys should stop jumping, too. 'Cause that would be polite of you."

Lucille and that Grace didn't pay attention to me.

That is how come I had to get back on the giant bed and shout in their faces.

"STOP JUMPING, I SAID! 'CAUSE I AM NOT ALLOWED TO JUMP! AND YOU GUYS SHOULDN'T JUMP, TOO!"

Grace springed way high in the air.

"Who's jumping? I'm not jumping," she said.

She giggled very silly. "I'm *bouncing!*"

Just then, my whole face got happy.

I hugged and hugged that girl.

'Cause Mother and Daddy didn't say I couldn't *bounce!*

After that, I bounced and bounced and bounced.

"BOUNCING...BOUNCING...BOUNC-ING ON THE GIANT BED," I sang.

I bounced till sweat came on my head.

Then I flopped down on the bed to rest.

I flopped on a plumpery pillow.

"Oooo, Lucille! This is the most

plumpery pillow I ever even saw!" I told her.

"Of *course* it is, silly," said Lucille. "That's because my nanna has all her pillows handmade in Sweden."

I quick swinged the plumpery pillow over to my friend Grace.

"Grace! Hey, Grace! Feel how plumpery this pillow is!" I said.

Only Grace didn't actually see it coming. And it accidentally hit her in the head.

I peeked at her under that thing.

"Yeah, only that did not even harm you, I bet. 'Cause plumpery pillows don't hurt people. Right, Grace. Right?"

That Grace did a teeny grin.

Then she took the plumpery pillow off her head. And she swinged it all around. And she hit me in the tummy!

"Ooomph!" I said.

Then I laughed and laughed.

"Hey! I was right! Plumpery pillows *don't* hurt people!"

After that, I hit Lucille in the head with my plumpery pillow. Plus also, I hit Grace again.

Then those guys got their own plumpery pillows. And all of us kept on hitting each other very fun!

Only just then, a mistake happened. 'Cause I didn't even know there was a rip in my plumpery pillow. And so the next time I hit Grace, all of my feathers exploded out of it!

There was a million bazillion of those floaty things.

They filled the whole air, practically.

Lucille did a gasp.

That Grace did a gasp, too.

I danced around very giggling.

"HEY! IT'S SNOWING!" I said. "IT'S SNOWING! IT'S SNO—"

Just then, the door swinged opened very fast!

It was Lucille's nanna!

She saw me holding the broken plumpery pillow!

My heart pounded hard inside of me.

"Hello," I said very nervous. "How are

you today? I am fine. Except I am having a little bit of a feather problem, apparently."

The nanna walked at me very slow.

Then she took my pillow out of my hands.

And she hided her face in that flatty thing.

And she didn't come out for a real long time.

7
Peeping

After a while, the nanna took us back to Lucille's room.

Me and Philip Johnny Bob got in our sleeping bag speedy fast.

Then that Grace got in her sleeping bag, too. And Lucille got into her softie bed.

"Not one more peep out of you girls," said the nanna very grouchy. "Do you hear me? Not one more *peep*."

She turned off the light and shut the door.

I stayed quiet a real long time. 'Cause I

was scared of that woman, that's why.

All of a sudden, I heard a teeny voice.

"Peep!" it said. "Peep, peep, peep!"

It was Lucille.

Me and that Grace giggled out loud at her.

"Peep," said that Grace.

"Peep," I said.

Peep, said Philip Johnny Bob.

Then pretty soon, all of us were peeping all over the place.

"Peep, peep, peep, *peep*. Peep, peep, peep, *peep*."

Lucille kept on peeping louder and louder and louder.

"PEEP! PEEP! PEEP!" she said.

Also, she was giggling very hard.

Finally, me and that Grace sat up in our sleeping bags. We stared at that girl.

"Lucille is peeping out of control," said that Grace.

"Maybe she is overly tired," I said. "Overly tired makes your brain go silly."

"PEEP!" said Lucille. "PEEP! PEEP! PEEP! PEEP! PEEP!"

Just then, Lucille's nanna opened the door again.

"SILENCE!" she yelled real scary.

Shivers came on my skin.

Then all of us quick crawled under our covers again.

And we closed our eyes.

And we didn't say another peep.

8
Morning

Morning came very early.

It was still dark outside.

I jiggled Lucille and that Grace.

"I'm hungry," I said. "Are you guys hungry. I am really, *really* hungry."

I shook them some more.

"Let's eat. You wanna eat? I really, *really* wanna eat."

Finally, Lucille and that Grace yawned and stretched.

Then all of us put on our bathrobes and

our slippers. And we went down the hall to get the nanna for breakfast.

Lucille shaked her real gentle.

"Wake up, Nanna," she whispered.

"Wake up, Nanna," said that Grace.

"Wake up, Nanna," I said.

The nanna did a snore.

That's how come we had to pull her up by her arms. And we turned a bright light in her face.

The nanna yawned real big.

It was not pleasant.

After that, she got her robe and slippers. And she went downstairs with us.

We sat at the long dining room table again.

The nanna passed out cereal bowls.

"Oh, Nanna! These are the brand-new china bowls you bought in France!

These are my favorites!" said Lucille.

All of a sudden, I felt a knot in my stomach again.

I tapped on the nanna's hand.

"Yeah, only here's the problem. I think I would like to have a plastic cereal bowl.

'Cause plastic is more my style."

The nanna rolled her eyes way up at the ceiling. I looked up there, too. But I didn't see anything.

"I don't *own* any plastic cereal bowls," she said.

After that, she brought in the orange juice. And she poured it into teeny crystal glasses.

I got down from my chair.

"Yeah, only guess what? I think I will just stand here and not eat. Or else I might spill something again," I said.

The nanna looked and looked at me.

Then she went into the kitchen and she brought me back a banana.

"Here. Try this," she said kind of nicer.

I did a smile.

Then I ate my banana very careful.

And I didn't spill a drop.

Mother picked me up at nine o'clock.

She came into the nanna's big, beautiful house to get me.

"My! What a lovely home you have here," she said to the nanna.

Then Mother walked to the big bowl of beautiful flowers. And she tried to smell those lovely things.

"NO! DON'T! THEY ARE JUST FOR SHOW PROBABLY!" I hollered.

After that, I said good-bye to my friends. And I thanked the nanna. And I quick pulled Mother out of that house. Or else she might break something, that's why.

I runned down the steps and got in my car. Then I rubbed my hand on the backseat.

It was not as soft as the nanna's backseat.

I smiled very relieved.

"It's good to be back," I said.

Mother drove down the long driveway.

My stomach growled real loud.

"Guess what? My tummy is still hungry for breakfast. 'Cause I didn't actually eat much this morning," I said.

Mother laughed.

"I swear, Junie B. Your stomach is a bottomless pit," she said.

Just then, another great idea popped into my head!

"Mother! Hey, Mother! Maybe you and me can stop at Grandma Miller's for breakfast! 'Cause she fixes blueberry pancakes every Sunday morning! And blueberry pancakes is my favorite breakfast in the whole entire world!"

Mother thought about my offer.

Then all of a sudden, she turned around the car. And we drove to my grandma Miller's house. And we were just in time for blueberry pancakes!

We ate a million bazillion of those delicious things!

Plus also I drank orange juice out of a plastic glass!

"Hurray!" I said. "Hurray for plastic!"

Then me and Grandma Miller hugged and hugged.

And guess what else?

I think I like my regular nanna just perfect.

Don't miss this next book about my **fun** in **kindergarten!**

Junie B. wants to be a beauty shop guy when she grows up. But first she needs a little practice. And a few volunteers. Is Junie B. on her way to a great new career? Or is she about to have the worst hair day ever?

Available Now!

Laugh yourself silly with

ALL the Junie B. Jones books!